MAGIC BROOM

Written by Michael J. Pellowski
Illustrated by Kathi Garry-McCord

Troll Associates

Library of Congress Cataloging in Publication Data

Pellowski, Michael.
    Magic broom.

    Summary: Brenda Bunny adopts a magic broom on the
condition it hide its magic from her parents, but
when a robber enters their home the broom reveals its
secret.
    [1. Brooms and brushes—Fiction. 2. Magic—Fiction.
3. Rabbits—Fiction] I. Garry-McCord, Kathleen, ill.
II. Title.
PZ7.P3656Mag   1986   [E]   85-14054
ISBN 0-8167-0636-0 (lib. bdg.)
ISBN 0-8167-0637-9 (pbk.)

10   9   8   7   6   5   4   3   2

MAGIC
BROOM

Deep in the woods was a little
house. It was a strange little
house. It looked spooky.

Who lived in the house? A little
old witch lived there long ago.
Then, one day, the witch went
away. And now the strange little
house was empty.

No one went near the house. It
looked strange. And it sounded
spooky. Strange, spooky sounds
came from the house.

There were banging sounds.
There were swishing sounds.
There were tapping sounds.
What made the sounds? No one
knew.

BANG!
Swish! Swish!
Tap! Tap! Tap!
The sounds frightened everyone.
Mr. Bunny was frightened.
"I will never go near *that* spooky
house," he said. "It's magic. And
I don't like magic."

Mrs. Bunny was frightened, too.
"I would never go up to that
door," she said. "That house is
strange. It is magic. And I don't
like magic."

The little house even frightened
Robber Fox.
"I would not go in there," said
Robber Fox. "Something magic
is in there. It is not a good house
to rob."

Something magic was in the empty house. Was it good magic? Was it bad magic? No one knew.

One day, little Brenda Bunny was playing in the woods. Hip-hop. She jumped along, deep into the woods. She was near the empty house. Brenda had never played there before.

Suddenly, a spooky sound came
from the house. BANG! Brenda
stopped playing.
"What was that?" she said.

There were more strange sounds.
Swish! Swish! Brenda looked
around.
"A little house!" she said. "It
looks like a little playhouse."

Brenda was not frightened. The
house did not look spooky to
her. She went up to the house.
Tap! Tap! Tap!

"Something is in the house," said
Brenda. "Something is tapping.
Maybe someone wants to come
out and play."

Brenda went to the door. It is not good to play in an empty house. Brenda knew that. She just wanted to know who was making those sounds.

Brenda opened the door. She did not go in. Brenda looked in.

What did she see? No one! The
house was empty. Only an old
broom stood in the corner.

"Only a broom," said Brenda.
"Then who made those sounds?"
BANG! Brenda looked at the
broom. The broom moved!

Swish! Swish! Up to the open
door swished the broom.
"A witch's broom," said Brenda.
"A magic broom. This is
spooky!"
But Brenda did not move.

Tap!
Tap! Tap!
Tap! Tap! Tap!
The broom danced before
Brenda. It wanted to go out. It
was not a spooky broom. It was
a playful broom.

The magic broom wanted to
play. It wanted to play with
Brenda. Brenda wanted to play,
too. Out they went.

"Let's play tag," said Brenda.
The broom tapped. It wanted to
play tag, too.
"Tag! You are it!" said Brenda.

Away ran Brenda. Swish! Away
flew the magic broom. Around
and around the woods they
went.

The broom tagged Brenda.
Brenda tagged the broom. Oh,
what fun they had playing tag.

"Now what will we play?" asked
Brenda. "I know. Hide-and-seek.
I will hide, and you will look
for me."

Tap! Tap! The magic broom
wanted to play. It did not look
while Brenda was hiding.
"Come and get me," shouted
Brenda.

Swish! Away the broom flew. It
looked here. It looked there. It
looked all around the woods.

"Here is where I am hiding,"
Brenda yelled.
Swish! The broom flew to
Brenda.
"I must go," the little bunny
said. "Day is over. Night is
coming. I must go home."

Brenda looked at the broom.
The broom tapped and swished.
It swished and tapped. It did
not like living in the empty
house. No one ever went near
the strange house.

"I had fun," Brenda said to the broom. "Would you like to go home with me? Would you like to live at my house? We could have fun every day."

Tap! Tap! Tap! The broom
wanted to go with Brenda.
"I will take you home," Brenda
said. "But do not do any magic.
My mother and father might not
like it."

34

Brenda flew home on the magic broom. High in the sky they flew. What a fun way to go home. Into the house went Brenda with the broom.

Mr. Bunny looked at Brenda.
Mrs. Bunny looked at Brenda.
"What is that?" asked Mr. Bunny.
"It is just an old broom," said
Brenda. "I am playing with it."

Days went by. Brenda and the
broom played every day. They
played in the woods. They
played and played.

At night, the broom stayed in
Brenda's house. It did not tap. It
did not bang or swish. The
broom did not make a sound. It
did not want to frighten Mr. and
Mrs. Bunny.

One night something strange
happened. *Creak*. The door to
the bunny house opened. A
stranger came in. He did not
make a sound. He looked
around.

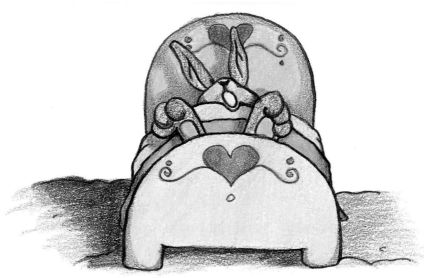

"Good," said the stranger. "Mr. Bunny is sleeping. Mrs. Bunny is sleeping. Everyone is sleeping. Now I can rob the house."

The stranger was Robber Fox.
He crept around the house
looking for something to rob.
What a bad, bad fox!
Robber Fox did not know about
Brenda's broom. Magic brooms
do not sleep. Magic brooms do
not like robbers. Out of its
hiding place flew the broom.

BANG! The broom hit Robber
Fox on the head. SWISH! It
tapped him on his bottom.
"Ouch!" yelled Robber Fox.
"Ouch! Ouch! Ouch!"

BANG! SWISH! TAP!
"Ouch! Ouch! Ouch!"
Robber Fox was very frightened.
"This house is strange!" he
yelled. "This house is spooky! It
has a magic broom."

"What is happening?" asked
Mr. Bunny.
"It is Robber Fox," said
Mrs. Bunny.
"My magic broom!" said Brenda.
"Stop it!" yelled Robber Fox.
"Ouch!"

Brenda's magic broom did not
stop. BANG! SWISH! It tapped
the robber from top to bottom.
Out the door ran Robber Fox.
"I am never coming near this
house again," he yelled.

Swish! The broom flew to Brenda.
"What a broom," said Mr.
Bunny. "It frightened Robber
Fox. But it does not frighten me.
I like its magic!"

Mrs. Bunny looked at the broom.
"What a good broom," she said.
"This magic broom is not strange
or spooky. A magic broom is
good to have around the house."

"I like you, magic broom," said
Brenda. "You do not have to
hide anymore. This is your home
now."
What did the broom say?
Bang! Swish!
Tap! Tap! Tap!